DATE DUE			
Oc 1 '90			
Oc 8 '90			
Ma 25 '92			
Ap 1 '92			
Ap 15 '92			
My 13 '92			
My 20 '92			
Ja 31 9			
Fe 9 96			
Fe 11 9			

4/30

F
NIL

Nilsson, Ulf.

If you didn't have
me.

RL: 4.5

IL: Ge 3-6

4/90 10.95

IMMANUEL LUTHERAN SCHOOL
MEMORIAL LIBRARY

If You Didn't Have Me

If You Didn't Have Me

Ulf Nilsson

Illustrated by Eva Eriksson

Translated from the Swedish
by Lone Thygesen Blecher
and George Blecher

Margaret K. McElderry Books
NEW YORK

F
NIL

Margaret K. McElderry Books
Macmillan Publishing Company
866 Third Avenue
New York, NY 10022
Collier Macmillan Canada, Inc.

First American edition 1987

Printed in the United States of America

10 9 8 7 6 5 4 3 2

Library of Congress Cataloging-in-Publication Data

Nilsson, Ulf.
   If you didn't have me.

   Translation of: Om ni inte hade mig.
   Summary: Spending most of a year with relatives on
a farm in southern Sweden while his parents are busy
building a new house in town, a young boy finds inner
strengths and unexpected sources of entertainment.
   [1. Farm life—Fiction.   2. Sweden—Fiction.
3. Self-reliance—Fiction]   1. Eriksson, Eva., ill.
II. Title.
PZ7.N589If   1987   [Fic]   86-21327
ISBN 0-689-50406-3

Composition by Fisher Composition, Inc.
New York, New York
Printed and bound by R. R. Donnelley & Sons
Harrisonburg, Virginia
Designed by Barbara A. Fitzsimmons

*Not everything is true
And most of it hasn't happened yet…*

Contents

If You Didn't Have Me

1

Alone in the Night

When I awoke it was quiet all around me. Quiet and dark. It was warm under the covers, but a cold draft came from the window next to the bed.

Outside, the night was pitch black. Though it was dark on the earth, there was some light in the sky, a faint, sad sort of light. Big clouds were floating above, waiting. Beyond the grass I could just make out the cherry tree and the old chicken coop.

I was at Grandma's house. It was the spring when my little brother and I lived with Grandma while Mama and Papa were building a house for us in town. It was May, and they had just finished digging the hole for the foundation and started pouring in the cement.

All alone and far, far away from Mama. When I got up, the floor was icy cold, so cold that I got goosebumps on my arms. I stood still listening until slowly I began to hear all the little sounds in Grandma's house.

The wall clock ticked slowly, haltingly. The small hand was between the four and five, and the big hand pointed to six. So it had to be four o'clock or five o'clock. Or six o'clock.

Grandma was asleep in the big bed in the next room. She muttered and mumbled in a thick, grumpy voice that I couldn't understand; she always talked in her sleep. Shivering, I ran in and stood by her bed. She wasn't wearing her glasses, so I could hardly recognize her. Could this be someone else's grandma?

Her face was wrinkled. Grooved like the bark of an old, old tree.

No, it was my grandma. There were her glasses on top of the Bible on the dresser. Next to them stood a glass of water, and in the glass were the teeth that she took out at night. Carefully I picked up the glass and held it against the faint light from the window. They looked like the teeth of a big fish splashing around in the water all by themselves. Shuddering, I put the glass down.

Grandma mumbled again. With her mouth fallen in, her lips looked strange. Underneath her eyelids her eyes moved back and forth. She growled like an old, old tiger. I missed Mama so badly. I wished I could crawl into her bed, into her warmth, and cuddle up under her arm with my back against her warm stomach. I didn't want to get into Grandma's bed! I was afraid to: She looked so different, almost ugly.

My little brother, who lay asleep in the small bed on the other side of the dresser, whimpered a bit. Suddenly he moved, hitting the mattress with his hand as he dreamed. He was lying on his stomach with his feet tucked up under him, and I wanted to lie behind him, pressed against the wall. He was as warm as fresh-baked bread.

But if I pushed in, he'd wake up right away.

I went back to my room and dressed in the dark as quickly as I could, fumbling under the bed for the rifle that Edwin had made for me. He'd cut the butt out of a board and fashioned the barrel from an old broomstick. The trigger was a nail.

With the rifle raised I walked into the kitchen. Grandma's rocking chair was standing motionless, and the radio next to it was silent. On the windowsill, the flies were asleep, and the bread and salt and sugar were standing in their usual places on the round table. The stove door rattled a little in the draft: The stove was cold.

I went into the front hall and stuck my feet into my cold wooden clogs. Then I opened the outside door. It opened inward, and was never locked. As I walked outside, cobwebs stuck to my face.

The yard was in darkness. The sky was gray and the big clouds hung quietly, waiting. Everything was still. With my rifle raised, I checked in all directions, but there was no sign of life anywhere. Edwin's room was dark. There was no light in Aunt Anna and Uncle Gustav's house, either. The window in the attic where my cousin Cilla slept was black.

I was alone. Completely alone. No life anywhere.

Then, far away, from down in the swamp, I heard a sound like a barking dog, a pitiful, lonely little dog. Or maybe it was a fox.

"It has to get light," I said quietly through chattering teeth.

Fear crept along my back like cold maggots.

As I walked past the barn door, the gravel crunched, and a crow who'd been sleeping in one of the poplar trees woke up and cawed sleepily. After I tightened my grip on the rifle, I felt less scared; I took aim at the crow but didn't shoot. It flew heavily to the other poplar.

I crept up to the chicken coop, opened the rusty latch, and looked in. Feathers ruffled, the chickens were roosting on their perches. It was quiet even in there—where it was usually so noisy. When I opened the door, a small gust of wind made some downy feathers float in the air like little clouds.

Who took care of everyone at night? No one was awake but me. But I wasn't afraid. I had my rifle. *I* was the one who took care of everyone.

"You don't have to be afraid," I said quietly to the chickens. "The fox is far, far away, all the way down in the swamp. And if he comes here I'll stop him."

I closed the door of the chicken coop and replaced the latch.

Then I snuck back toward the barn. On my way I passed the sheep shed, but only looked in through the window. In the far corner, the lambs looked like big balls of fluff.

The hinges of the barn door screeched as I pulled it open. Inside, the air was heavy with heat, which rushed out into the cold spring morning like a cloud of steam. Inside the barn a piglet grunted; then all was quiet again. I crept up to the pigpen. The piglets lay pressed against their mamas' big, soft bellies. They panted, and the sows snored heavily.

"You don't have to be afraid," I said quietly.

The windows were misted over. A fuzzy moth buzzed against a pane, trying to get out. The motion of its wings sent tiny drops of water flying all around.

I walked up to the boar's stall. There he lay, so heavy that he seemed to have flowed out all over the floor and become the same shape as his stall. In one corner lay his head with the ears covering his face as though he didn't want to see anything. In the other corner I saw his tail sticking up, straight and powerful, like a rhubarb stalk.

That boar wasn't afraid of anything. You could kill him, my Uncle Gustav said, and he *still* wouldn't be afraid!

Past the boar's stall was the door to the mill where my uncle ground the grain to make grits for the pigs. He emptied the grain sacks into a big funnel, which stood directly over an electric motor attached to a mill. After the grain was ground up into grits, it was emptied into sacks below.

It made so much dust! The dust whirled around and stuck to the walls and the floor in heavy drifts, making everything look big and soft and strange. Someone's forgotten clogs on the floor looked as if they'd fit a giant. The hammer on the bench was as big as a sledgehammer, and the empty sacks hanging on the wall looked like puffy ghosts. My Uncle Gustav said that the rats and mice feasted on the grain every night, but all I saw were thousands of little tracks in the grain dust on the floor.

Edwin's gloves were hanging on a hook. I put them on. They were so big that they slipped off by themselves. When I took them off, my hands smelled funny.

I walked into the main room of the barn. The horse was standing stock-still, sleeping. Only his huge chest moved now and then, and the hair around his nostrils trembled.

The cows were lying on their beds of straw. I stopped next to Bella and carefully patted the smooth skin on her cheek. She started, her skin shuddering as though she were shaking off a stubborn fly.

The cows breathed heavily, heavily.

"Never be afraid," I whispered.

A cat jumped down softly from a low beam, mewed quietly and slipped between my legs. As I went out, she followed me, purring more and more affectionately and rubbing herself against me. I sat down in the grass, which felt damp through my pants. I was not alone anymore: Now

it was me and the cat. Everything else was asleep,
everything else was quiet, nighttime. The fox had
stopped barking.

The cat crept into my lap.

"It has to get light!" I said to the cat. "It has to
get light and bright."

Didn't it seem a little lighter?

A bird started to sing its first drowsy morning
serenade.

"All of you, sing!" I said.

And they did start to sing, one after another!
From the blackberry bushes with their tiny leaves,

from the cherry tree with its bursting buds, there was singing everywhere! I sat still, petting the cat.

"Now it has to get light, bright and light."

And beyond the chicken coop it did grow lighter.

"It has to get light, light, light!" I said.

The crow scolded peevishly from the bare, spindly poplar. A sheep bleated in its pen.

The cat and I sat quite still. I was afraid to move.

"Light, light, light," I said quietly.

And the light beyond the chicken coop grew clearer and clearer. Singing their songs, the larks rose into the sky.

"Sing, sing, sing," I said.

And they sang and they sang.

"Sun, come out," I said.

I punched my fist into the wet grass.

"Sun, come out!"

And the sun came out. It peeked timidly between the chicken coop and the tractor shed, from beyond the fields and the woods.

The sun pricked my eyes.

"More, more, more," I shouted.

I put the cat down and started dancing wildly in the grass—around and around and around and around. The cat closed her eyes and licked her paws.

Now I could see half the sun above the fields.
My legs were tired, and I was out of breath.

"Did you see that!" I said to the cat, lifting her
under her arms into the air. She hissed, slipped
softly out of my hands into the grass and trotted
off proudly under the currant bushes, never looking back at me.

Then Uncle Gustav's window shade shot up
with a clatter.

I felt a faint breeze. I was tired and completely
dizzy.

The big, fat clouds drifted silently toward the
sea. A flock of seagulls screeched mournfully to
each other; they looked as though they were pulling the clouds on long, invisible strings.

Now the day had started!

2

If You Didn't Have
Me . . .

Grandma was still asleep. My little brother lay on his stomach, rubbing his head back and forth on the pillow; that meant he would wake up soon.

Quietly I closed the door to the kitchen. I wanted to surprise them both.

"When you wake up, I'll have real food for you."

For breakfast Grandma ate bread and butter, and she drank coffee. Little Brother drank milk from a bottle, regular cold milk. I usually had bread and butter, and I drank milk—at Grandma's, that is—for this was the spring when my little brother and I lived at Grandma's while

11

Papa and Mama were building a house in town. Building a house takes a really long time. At home with my Mama I always got hot chocolate. . . .

First, I opened the door of the wood-burning stove and looked inside. It was completely cold, and a draft was sending little flakes of soot spinning up the chimney.

"I'll make a fire for Grandma and heat up the coffee."

But could I do it? At home we didn't have a wood-burning stove; ours was electric. All you had to do was turn a knob.

How did Grandma do it? I didn't usually get up in the morning with her, and by the time I woke up, a fire was already burning in the stove. Every once in a while Grandma would put in more wood or a charcoal briquette.

She'd always warn me not to touch the door, or I'd burn myself.

But how did she start the fire when the stove was cold? Next to the stove stood a little pile of firewood. The charcoal briquettes were in a bucket, and in the corner were kindling and some old newspapers. The matches were on a shelf.

Grandma was always talking about how much she liked the charcoal briquettes—they gave off a lot of heat, she said. So I took one from the bucket and put it into the stove. Then I took the matchbox and struck a match. When I put it in the stove the flame fluttered in the draft; it licked at the briquette, but nothing happened.

I lit another match. That didn't work either. I lit one after the other, but when the box was empty the briquette still lay as cold as a lump of iron in the middle of the stove with many burned matches around it.

A little coffee was left in the pot. Even if it was cold, at least Grandma would have her coffee.

"She can have a little more sugar instead! That'll make her happy!"

Grandma kept her china cups and saucers on the lower shelves of the sideboard. I liked to sit and look at the cups; I thought they were so beautiful—white, with a blue stripe and a gold stripe.

I took out a cup and saucer and poured the cold coffee from the pot. Grandma used two lumps of sugar, but I decided to give her three, or why not four?

"Don't be stingy! Give her five!"

I put the coffee on a tray. Now for the bread! There was a big round loaf on the table, which Grandma cut by holding it against her chest. The bread knife was lying next to it; it was very sharp. I was afraid to cut the bread the way Grandma did, so I just put the knife on the loaf and started sawing. Slowly and laboriously, the knife worked its way through the bread like sawing wood. The first slice was as thick as the heel of a wooden clog at one end, and at the other as thin as a knife.

"I'll eat this one myself."

The next one would be for Grandma. I set the bread on its end and sawed away. At the beginning it came out fairly thick and even, but halfway through the knife came out and broke off the bread, leaving only half a slice. I went on sawing the other half. This one was like a small axhead too, but not as bad as the first. When I put them next to each other, the two halves fit nicely.

"I'll stick them together with butter!"

Since the butter was in the pantry, I put on my clogs again and went to get it. The pantry door stuck at the bottom; I kicked it open and went down the half flight of stairs. On the shelves were flour and potatoes and carrots and black bread and milk and bacon and herring, and on the floor was a big mousetrap. The spring was taut, and the little piece of cheese was just waiting for some poor mouse. I made a wide circle around it.

The butter crock was on the top shelf. I climbed up and took it down. Then I looked for the cheese and sausage, but I couldn't find them anywhere. The only cheese in sight was the little piece in the mousetrap.

"That means that Grandma won't have anything but butter on her bread!"

When I got back to the kitchen, I found that the butter was so hard from the cold that it broke into big lumps when I tried to spread it; the bread stuck to the lumps and then fell apart, until there were holes all over the slice of bread and big lumps of butter and bread. Finally I stuck the two halves of Grandma's slice together with a lump of butter. It looked very good. I had used a lot of butter.

"Well, at least butter is *delicious*!"

It was too bad that there wasn't anything else to put on the bread. I decided to use a few pieces of sugar—they were better than nothing. But there were still two big holes, one in Grandma's slice and one in mine, that I couldn't do anything about. If I filled them I'd use all the butter. . . .

I went outside to the garden. Strong, green grass had begun to sprout. Dandelions were everywhere, and along the wall of the house grew nettles and crocuses.

"I'll take two crocuses. Two blue ones."

I stuck them into the two holes in the bread.

Now the sandwiches looked very beautiful. They made me so hungry that my mouth started to water.

I filled my glass and my little brother's bottle with milk, put everything on the tray, and went in to surprise Grandma and Little Brother.

Grandma had just woken up. She looked like herself again—her glasses were on her nose, and the glass on the dresser was empty. When Grandma smiled at me her mouth looked normal again.

"Little one, are you up already?"

"I've taken care of all the animals," I said.

"I've kept them safe from the fox. And I have a surprise for you."

"Oh, my! And it isn't even my birthday."

I put the tray on the dresser. My little brother awoke, and I gave him his bottle.

Grandma put on panties and slips and things like that. There were buckles and buttons and belts everywhere. Then she pinned up her hair.

"What a fine job you've done," she said. "Coffee and bread and a beautiful flower."

"Go ahead and eat it! It's very good. . . ."

I drank my milk and ate from the thinnest end of my bread. Grandma took a tiny, tiny sip of her coffee.

"Ah, that's good," she said. "But we'd better get a fire going in the stove, anyway."

She started toward the kitchen door. My little brother whimpered.

"Mama, come! Come now!"

"There, there, you're doing just fine," said Grandma, and she walked out. She took some paper, wadded it into a ball and stuffed it into the stove. On top she laid some small sticks and kindling. She took a new box of matches out of the kitchen cabinet.

"You can't light the charcoal briquette directly. But you'll learn soon enough. It just takes a little practice." *She* started the fire with one match!

Then she went back to her room, sat down on the bed, and picked up her piece of bread. When she lifted it, it collapsed.

"I used a lot of butter," I said. "It tastes very good."

"Oh, yes, it's just the way it should be."

I sat on the floor by my little brother's bed, singing quietly to myself:

> *If you didn't have me*
> *You'd have so much to do.*
> *If you didn't have me*
> *Who'd save the animals*
> *And make a little food?*
> *If you didn't have me.*

In the kitchen stove the fire crackled, the coffee water bubbled, and Grandma sat at the table, trying to trim the bread and smooth out the butter. She'd found the cheese in the pantry.

> *If you didn't have me*
> *Who'd make the food?*

"What a clever boy you are," she said.

But I heard her pour the sweet, cold coffee down the drain.

3

I'm in Charge
of the Spring

It was the end of May the spring my little brother
and I lived at Grandma's while Papa and Mama
were building a house for us in town. They had
just started putting up the walls.

Uncle Gustav owned the farm, and Edwin was
his hired hand.

In the mornings they milked the cows together.
Then they ate breakfast with my aunt. The rest of
the day each had his own jobs to do. Uncle
Gustav went off in the tractor. Sometimes he
went out to harrow the fields. In the distance you
could see the little red tractor working its way

19

across the pastures, trailing a cloud of dust. Sometimes he drove to the Farmers' Cooperative in town and traded a whole load of sacks for another equally large load. This spring he was busy digging drainage ditches in the swamp.

Edwin's job was to take care of the barn. And I went along with him.

While he let the cows out to graze, I carried a long stick and made sure that they didn't wander into the road. When a cow got too close I'd holler, "Whoa, whoa, whoa," and wave my stick. The big, slow cow would break into a gallop, which made the ground thunder and shake.

"Whoa, whoa, whoa," I'd shout happily.

When the cows were safely in the pasture, we'd walk back and Edwin would clean out the stalls. Each one had to be scraped completely clean. Then all the cow patties had to be shoveled down the middle aisle and onto the big manure pile behind the barn.

Feeding the pigs was next. All the different kinds of feed had to be measured carefully.

"If they get too much of the grits they'll get too fat, see? You have to figure it out exactly. Five times five. Do you know how much that makes?"

I shook my head.

"Twenty-five. If you make a mistake they'll all

20

get as fat as the boar. Or as skinny as sticks."

I stored it away in the back of my mind.

Edwin shoveled grits into the troughs and I walked behind, giving each pig a few potatoes. Their snouts were white from the grit flour; they gobbled and slobbered, and when they bit into the big potatoes juice squirted out of their mouths.

Then the chickens had to be fed. And the sheep in their enclosure needed water. And the horse had to be taken care of. And the rabbits needed new straw in their cages and dandelion leaves to eat. And a chicken had to be slaughtered. And a cow that was being kept inside had to be checked over; something had to be done about her udder inflammation. And the horse's coat had to be currycombed and its hooves cleaned out.

There was so much to do.

When the morning chores in the barn were over, there were many other things to do.

A board in the gate needed to be replaced. A windowpane was broken. On the south side of the house the gable needed to be repainted.

Then there was the garden. The potatoes must be mounded up. The berry bushes needed more fertilizer, and everything had to be watered.

I followed behind Edwin all the time. There

was so much to do. So much. And when all this was done there were still a few hours till noon. Edwin picked up the long hoe and walked down to the beet field at the edge of the woods.

I lay down in the tall grass. Edwin started to hoe.

"I'm going to weed out all the small plants. All the weeds have to go, and I'll leave just the healthy plants."

Stooped over, he walked through the field, his

hoe moving as fast as a drumstick. A string of dandelions, crabgrass, and skinny beet plants landed in between the rows. Only fine, big beet plants were left standing.

"You have so much to take care of," I said.

"It's a big responsibility," Edwin said.

"Isn't it hard?"

"Well, that's what life's about, see, having responsibility."

"But isn't it *hard?*"

Edwin laughed. By now he'd worked his way far into the field.

"Five times five," he shouted.

"Twenty . . . is that right?"

"Twenty-five! When you can manage that, you'll be all right. . . . I'm weeding out the dandelions. And I don't want that ugly goosefoot, either. This one's a good plant, but that scrawny one has to go."

He vanished into the distance. I could hear that he was talking, but not what he was saying. I stayed in the grass, chewing on a dandelion.

"Five times five is twenty-five. . . ."

I'm the one who takes care of *everything*. I'm the one who takes care of the whole spring, I said to myself. I'm the one who says when everything should begin. I'm the one who makes sure that everything gets done.

I lay on my back and looked up at the clouds. One big cloud and fifteen small ones were drifting out to sea.

"That's good," I said. "Keep going!"

I gave them names so that I could tell them what to do. The biggest one was Big Carl. Behind him came Peter and Little Hot Dog.

"That's right, Little Hot Dog. Good!"

High above them was a long, thin cloud that moved much more slowly than the others. I called it Fuzzy.

"Full speed ahead, Fuzzy, don't be a slow-poke!"

Behind me the trees grew close together. The beeches had pale green leaves, but the big oak trees were still bare.

I named the oak trees Torsten and Rutger.

"Torsten and Rutger, you can start now! Go ahead! Start growing leaves! That's it, that's good, very good!"

I named the beeches Signe and Belinda and In-galill.

"Get going, girls! Grow some little twigs! You can grow your boughs a little thicker, too, but just a little. . . ."

Fuzzy was still behind the others.

"Come on, speed it up, we don't have all day!"

24

I had to take care of the bushes, too. But what were the ones with the tiny leaves called? And, next to them, the ones with the white flowers? I didn't know the names of either.

So I called them Fluff 1, Fluff 2, Fluff 3, all the way to Fluff 1000: Those were the bushes with the tiny green leaves.

"All you Fluffs, you can start blooming now! Any color you want. . . ."

I could call the ones with the white flowers something like White Bubbles or White Lightning. But White Lightning wouldn't do; that meant something else. How about White Mishmash? There were only four of that kind, anyway.

It felt wonderful to be the one who took care of everything. You could just lie there in the grass chewing on a dandelion and decide everything. You were the boss.

"I'm the one who's in charge of the spring," I said proudly.

Then I noticed that Fuzzy wasn't moving at all. Little Hot Dog and Peter were already far away on the horizon.

I had to do something about this! And Rutger and the other oak tree—whatever his name was—hadn't done a thing. Still completely bare.

"Hmmm, I'll remember this," I said sternly.

But actually, I didn't have time for them any longer. I looked into the grass next to me. Things were in a terrible mess.

From a distance it looked just like ordinary grass, but up close there were actually about twenty different kinds of flowers and leaves. One kind had just started to poke out of the ground with two penny-sized leaves. Another had long, skinny shoots, a third had flowers. On the fourth the flowers had died and seed pods were forming.

Everything was growing busily. Twenty different kinds. And at least a hundred of each kind. And that was just in the small spot where I was lying. And all of them needed names: I didn't even have that many names in my head. Then I looked closer at my plants. Ants were scurrying all over among the leaves. The boss of the spring ought to be the boss of them, too. Give them names, tell them what to do and then make sure it's done properly.

I started to sweat.

And it wasn't just ants. Spiders were also scampering across the dry leaves closest to the ground. Flies were buzzing. Bumblebees and honeybees too—and in the dandelions there were tiny black beetles.

26

I looked inside a dandelion. The flower was made up of a thousand little petals. Green petals held up the flower, and inside those was a circle of yellow ones. Then there was a layer of delicate little petals with cleft ends that curled into themselves. And in the very center a bristly yellow mat. That was where the beetles were crawling around. What they were doing only they seemed to know—no boss knew, that was for sure.

There was so much to do. So much.

And here I was sitting and wasting my time on a forgotten little spot at the edge of the woods when there were many more important things to do at home with the carrots, flowers, and apple trees!

I ran home as fast as I could, bolting across the field. My heart was beating hard in my chest, I was in a tizzy and didn't know where to begin; I had more to do than the salesclerk at the Farmers' Cooperative.

Of course, Edwin was the one who was in charge of the carrots. He could just as well keep on doing that.

And Grandma took care of the flowers.

After them, the apple and cherry trees were the most important.

Panting, I stood under the largest apple tree.

Millions of apple blossoms billowed above me; on every twig far, far above me, halfway to heaven, flowers were blossoming. Honeybees and bumblebees buzzed all over the tree, thousands of them hurrying in and out of millions of flowers. And every single trip in and out of the white flowers was necessary—or else there would be no apples in the fall.

On each skinny little branch, there was more traffic than in the ferry station in the city. And I had to be the stationmaster of everything. And be the boss of all the leaves and flowers, too!

Exhausted, I sat down under the tree. It buzzed and hummed, and I was so tired I almost fell asleep. Someone else would have to be in charge. I'd had enough!

After lunch when all of us were drinking coffee under Grandma's arbor, I told them the whole story.

Uncle Gustav laughed like a horse. Grandma said, "There are some things that people are in charge of. But there are others that we'd better leave to our Lord. Oh yes, that's for sure!"

Edwin said, "It all takes care of itself, that's what's so amazing, see! Every single bumblebee knows what it's supposed to do. That's how life works. That's what makes the bumblebee's life worth living, see!"

In the apple tree next to us the bumblebees kept buzzing. And the honeybees hummed. Just one endless, tireless buzzing and humming.

4

Alone with
the Chickens and the Pigs

One day my Grandma had to go to the hospital to see Dr. Engman for a checkup. She'd had a hernia operation, and now Dr. Engman wanted to make sure that it had healed properly.

My aunt was taking her to town, and my little brother was going with them.

They had a 10:15 appointment.

"At Dr. Engman's you have to wait forever," my Uncle Gustav said. "Once I got well before I even saw him. Luckily I had time enough to get sick again while I was waiting. Ha ha ha."

*   *   *

This was at the beginning of June the summer that my Papa and Mama were building a house in town. By now they said that the ground floor was finished.

My uncle had hired a bulldozer to finish digging the drainage ditches in the swamp. Uncle Gustav and Edwin had packed a lunch and were getting ready to leave—they expected to be gone all day helping the bulldozer operator.

"But who will feed the chickens and the piglets?" Edwin said. "They've got to be fed and watered, you know."

"Cilla will have to do it," said Uncle Gustav.

Cilla was my cousin. Her summer vacation had just started. She was a few years older than me and would have nothing to do with me; all she wanted to do was to lie on her bed in her room in the attic reading books all day long.

"Why do *I* have to do it?" she shouted crossly from the attic. "Do you expect me to ruin my whole vacation?"

"But someone has to feed the piglets and chickens, see."

Cilla stuck her head out the window and glared down at me. "The little pip-squeak could do that. It's a job for babies, anyway. . . . Doesn't he ever have to do *anything?*"

*　　*　　*

So it was decided. Grandma made sandwiches for my lunch and then everyone left. Cilla curled up in her room in the attic and read books.

I sat waiting in Grandma's rocking chair. When both hands of the old clock were pointing straight up, I was supposed to go out and feed the chickens and the pigs.

I rocked and rocked and rocked. The clock ticked slowly, and one of the hands went around and around. But the two hands didn't point up at the same time. . . .

While I waited, I ate a sandwich. Then I rocked and rocked and rocked some more.

I ate another sandwich.

I was waiting just to do a baby job—that's what Cilla had called it. Just a stupid little job that babies could do. I started to get really mad. I rocked so furiously that the runners clattered against the floor.

Then I leafed through one of Grandma's newspapers. It was the *Pentecostal Times,* and there were pictures of Jesus, poor children, and scary lions in Africa.

In one picture they had caught a lion in a big cage.

Wouldn't that be something! To feed a lion! To sneak up close to the cage and open the door, rifle in hand. And the lion would roar so loud you'd have to cover your ears. I'd just say: "If you don't keep quiet, you won't get any food."

And when the lion was completely quiet, I'd give him the pieces of meat. And then of course he'd be so grateful, and he'd think that I was very brave. And after that he and I would be the best of friends. Even though everyone else was scared of him.

Feeding a lion, wouldn't that be something!

But feeding the chickens and piglets! Nothing but a stupid little job for babies!

Both hands were pointing straight up. I ate the last sandwich and went outside.

The sun was as bright as in Africa. A rooster crowed. Far off in the swamp I could hear the stubborn growl of a bulldozer. Or was it a hungry lion?

In the chicken yard the chickens were walking around, pecking at the ground. The yard was surrounded by a tall wire fence with a latched door. At the far end was a fence of unpainted boards, and on the other side of the fence the piglets were rooting and grunting. The chickens could decide for themselves when they wanted to be outside. If they wanted to go back in they could walk through a small door in the chicken coop. They couldn't get over the tall fence, and they had no interest in jumping over the wooden fence to the piglets.

In the barn I filled a bucket with grain for the chickens and a bucket of grits for the piglets. Then I gripped them tightly and staggered toward the chicken yard.

As I opened the door to the chickens, who walked around clucking mournfully, they jumped aside in fright. I closed the door behind me. But then a big hen with cropped tail feathers noticed that I was carrying food. She came closer and looked me over carefully, cocking her head to one side.

I put down the bucket with the pig food and got ready to scatter the chicken feed. That's the way Edwin always did it, and that's the way it had been done every single day that I had been there. But then the big hen with the cropped tail feathers rushed up to the pig feed and poked into the grits, making the bucket rattle!

She wasn't supposed to do that! If she ate the pig food everything would go wrong! She might get sick and die. And I wouldn't have any pig food left. What would the pigs eat? They'd get a stomachache from the chicken feed!

The chickens would die, the pigs would get stomachaches—and everything would be my fault!

* * *

The big hen with the cropped tail stood with half her body stuffed into the bucket. I said, "You can't do that. Get out this instant!"

Carefully, using one finger, I tried to get her out of the bucket. Then I used my whole hand. Her neck was as taut and hard as a steel wire; I couldn't budge her an inch.

Then I tried to drive her away with my foot, but her powerful claws gripped the ground.

I was about to start crying.

Finally I lifted the bucket as high as I could, and she hit her head against the bucket handle. Her face was white with flour as she clucked angrily at me.

Now I was holding one bucket in each hand. I raised them as high as I could. Then I noticed that all the chickens were coming toward me. The ones who weren't already outside were crowding to get through the little door of the coop. At first they came slowly and uncertainly, their heads cocked, their red combs flapping. Their cold, unblinking eyes stared at me as they got closer and closer, and their beaks looked hard and sharp.

Now they had surrounded me on all sides. They were cold and strange-looking. They wanted to eat all their own food and the pigs' food, too. And maybe me as well. . . .

The big hen with the cropped tail feathers was their leader—there must have been fifty or a hundred of them. She walked in front, and when she began pecking at the bucket the others grew brave enough to do it, too. They stretched their necks to reach over the top of the bucket, and didn't even seem to notice me anymore. I stood motionless, scared to death.

When I felt their hard, cold feet on my toes as they clambered over my sandals, I screamed. They paused for just a moment, cocked their heads to the opposite side and stared stiffly at me with their glassy eyes.

I ran as fast as I could to the wooden fence; the pigs would protect me!

I climbed onto the fence with the chickens behind me. They gathered in a cluster below me, waiting. Laughing with relief, I jumped down to the piglets.

But there it was even worse.

Twenty-five hungry piglets came rushing out of the muck—splattering mud all over, and sliding toward me.

I was about to start crying again. Usually when I came close to them they were scared to death and ran away. But now it was just the opposite.

Maybe *they* were as hungry as lions?

They grunted and tried to knock me over to get at the food in the buckets, and they stepped on my toes with their wet, hard trotters. I backed up against the fence and set the two buckets on the highest slat. Then I climbed carefully up myself. There I stood, on a board only about four inches wide, with a bucket on either side of me. The sun was still as hot as Africa.

Below me on one side of the fence were twenty-five hungry, angry piglets, shoving one another, pushing to get closer, trying to reach me on top of the fence. On the other side, as still as vultures, stood hundreds of chickens just waiting for me to fall.

If only I'd had my rifle with me. . . .

I sat down on the narrow board. I couldn't do a thing. I was trembling, and it probably wouldn't be long before I fell down from sheer exhaustion.

That would be the end of me. . . .

I waited and waited.

I called for my cousin Cilla hundreds of times, but of course she was just lying on her bed reading books. I wished that Grandma would come home, but she was probably still sitting in Dr. Engman's waiting room.

The chickens and pigs just stared at me; they were waiting, too.

Now and then a chicken got tired of waiting and started scratching in the ground for worms. And once in a while one of the piglets took a turn around the sty and splashed in the mud.

Otherwise, nothing happened. I just got more and more tired. Sooner or later I'd fall off the fence—either to the chickens or the pigs. . . .

Then suddenly I saw Edwin walking along in the outside yard, carrying a spade; he hadn't seen me yet. Then I noticed that the lion had stopped growling in the swamp.

I called to him in a pitiful little voice.

He came up to the fence and looked at me for a long time. He seemed to be smiling slightly.

"What should I do?" I squeaked.

"Have you been there long?" he asked.

"All day," I answered. "What should I do? What should I do?"

"Throw the pig food to the pigs," he said, "and the chicken feed to the chickens. That's what they're waiting for, see?"

I knocked one of the buckets into the pigpen and the other into the chicken yard. The animals threw themselves at the food, the pigs grunting and snorting, the chickens clucking happily.

Not one of them looked up at me. None of them cared about me at all. I felt hurt.

I climbed down into the pigpen and picked up the bucket and gave it to Edwin. The pigs paid no attention to me. They just gobbled up their food. I climbed over the fence to the chickens and picked up that bucket, too. They didn't pay any attention to me, either.

Edwin gave me the water hose and I filled their water troughs. Then I left the yard and closed the latch.

"Were you afraid of them?" he asked.

I nodded.

In the evening after Grandma had come back from Dr. Engman (who had found that everything had healed as it was supposed to), we all sat under the arbor.

"That was no baby job," I said. "If my little brother had walked in there, they would've eaten him up, I promise you!"

The cat was sitting under the table licking her paws very, very carefully.

"There are no baby jobs," said Edwin. "They

just don't exist, see."

"Was he afraid of the chickens?" asked
Grandma. "Oi, oi, oi, boys shouldn't be afraid of
chickens!"

"He isn't anymore," Edwin said.

"That's good to hear. Very, very good!"

5

The Stagecoach

My little brother and I were allowed to ride in the back of the wagon to the Farmers' Cooperative in town. Uncle Gustav drove the tractor that pulled the wagon, and we lay in the back end, looking out over the edge. I held on to my little brother's pants so that he wouldn't fall out.

The ground flew past below us. The tall grass slapped against the wheel axle, and stood wavering for a long time afterward.

It was already that part of summertime when the grass was taller than my little brother—during the summer when my Mama and Papa were building a house in town. They were just putting in the second-story floor; Papa was nailing the under-flooring to the crossbeams.

When you lie in the back of a wagon and look down at the ground, the speed makes you dizzy. You can see dandelions and clover appear and disappear in the narrow strip of grass in the middle of the road. And if you just stare down, there's no way of knowing where you're going, no matter how hard you try. . . .

At the Farmers' Cooperative Olofsson was the boss. He decided everything. All day long he'd strut around with his thumbs in his belt, looking important.

After we arrived, Uncle Gustav talked prices with him for a while. They were deciding how much twenty sacks were worth.

Then we went to the cashier and paid. The cashier had a black coat and big stacks of paper money on which all the pictures of old men were staring in the same direction. He flipped through the stacks, counting faster than anyone else could do. The room smelled of dust and old money.

Afterward we drove the tractor and hay wagon to the warehouse. Down there Old Johan and his son Paul worked hauling the sacks.

Olofsson joined us, thundering and growling.

"Give him twenty sacks. And be quick about it!"

"Be quick about it, yes sir, yes sir!" said Old Johan.

Panting, he ran off for the sacks.

"We can't do it any faster than we can do it," Paul said. "We've got plenty to do already."

Paul was the exact opposite of his father. He had a dark look about him, and he moved slowly, as if he were walking in water. My little brother was scared of him, and started to cry.

Paul just laughed.

Olofsson slammed the door behind him.

Paul yelled, "If you'd only pick up a sack every once in a while, I'd take care of the rest!"

But Olofsson had already left.

"Which sacks do you want?" Paul asked me. "Oh, I don't suppose you know that."

He was so angry that his wad of chewing tobacco started to slip out of the pocket in his lip.

As Paul walked slowly into the storeroom, Old Johan came out carrying a heavy, heavy sack which he hoisted onto the hay wagon; it shook under the weight.

"Don't worry about the boy. He's in a bit of a bad mood. . . . We'll be going home for lunch soon, then he'll cheer up."

Old Johan's face and hair were both white.

44

Whether it was from flour or age you couldn't tell.

"Which sacks did you say you wanted?" It was Paul shouting from the storeroom.

My Uncle Gustav just laughed.

On our way home we drove past the swamp where the big bulldozer was standing all alone in the field. Maybe the driver was on his lunch break.

I called out, and Uncle Gustav stopped. My little brother and I slid off and walked over to look at the big machine. The tractor drove home without us.

We walked up to the bulldozer and climbed the muddy steps. The door to the driver's cabin was open, so we went inside.

I put my little brother behind the wheel. He hummed and vroomed until the spit flew. We didn't dare touch all the switches and knobs— what if the machine started up and bolted across the fields and meadows, digging up things as it went?

We climbed down again and went to look at the big scoop. It was as big as a house, and its lower teeth were like elephant tusks. We crawled inside.

As we were sitting there, we heard voices coming closer. Singing, hooting, noisy voices. There were at least four of them: One made funny sounds and yelled, "Bang, bang," another howled like a dog, a third sang, and the fourth screamed, "Stupid, stupid!"

I looked out of the scoop, and my heart started beating wildly. It was the kids who lived in the woods. Everyone knew about them. They were Old Johan's kids, Paul's younger brothers. They didn't care *whom* they beat up!

Cilla had told me that they fought like wildcats. They'd pull your pants down and tie the legs in so many knots that you couldn't get them untied again. They were killers, that's what they were.

What were we going to do? Thoughts rushed around in my head like frightened mice.

We made ourselves as small as possible.

I whispered, "We have to be quiet now. Otherwise they'll kill us. . . ."

I was hoping that they hadn't seen me.

But they had.

"Look!" one of them yelled. "Some stupid idiots are sitting inside the scoop."

The second voice howled, the third one shouted, "Bang, bang," and the fourth one screamed, "Stupid, stupid!"

Then it was quiet for a while. They were probably whispering about what they were going to do to us. Once they'd tied seven knots in one single cap. It could never be used for anything after that except maybe as a ball, Cilla had said.

What were they up to?

Cilla had told me that they were really dangerous. They'd attack anyone. They thought that farmers should be beaten up, and that children of farmers should *really* be beaten up! They weren't farmers, they were workers. And that was very different. If you were a worker, then your job was to beat up farmers. That's what Cilla had said.

What *were* they up to?

Bang! A big rock came flying at us full speed. It hit the scoop and made the metal ring. Then came another rock, and another, and another after that. The sounds clanged inside the scoop like a church bell. My little brother began to cry.

I hugged him as hard as I could.

"Don't be afraid, don't be afraid," I whispered.

Our ears were ringing. And then more rocks, and the scoop boomed and clanged and I could hear their coarse laughter. My little brother held his ears and squeaked like a train whistle.

"I'll always protect you, Little Brother."

But how was I going to protect him? I tried to peek out around the edge of the scoop and shout for them to stop. But two rocks came flying at me, just missing my head.

Quickly I crept back inside. Now they started

to come closer. They were picking up even bigger rocks from the field; when the rocks hit the scoop they sounded like thunder. I held my ears, but no matter how hard I pressed, the sounds squeezed in. It felt as though everything inside my head was shaking, too.

Then suddenly I saw someone on the road riding by on a big bicycle. I grabbed my little brother's hand and ran out.

"Stop!" I yelled. "Stop! Stop! Stop!"

But the boys just laughed and threw stones that whistled around our ears.

We ran back inside the scoop. The thunder was worse than ever.

"I'll protect you," I comforted my brother. "I'll always protect you, Little Brother!"

At least the person cycling on the road had seen us.

Carefully I peeked out.

It was Paul! It was their own big brother Paul! We couldn't expect any help from him! More than likely he'd go and get even bigger rocks to throw at the scoop. After that, I didn't think my little brother and I would ever be able to hear again.

Paul stopped the bike and walked up to his brothers. He didn't do what I thought he'd do.

"What do you think you're doing?" he said grumpily.

Then he gave each in turn a slap on the face. The youngest one, the one who kept saying "Stupid, stupid," got such a hard push that he ended up sitting on the ground.

I crept out with my little brother.

"What kind of stupid thing is this?" Paul said. "You don't *do* this kind of thing!"

The smallest one, the one sitting in the meadow, said, "But it was just for fun."

"Well, it's not very funny!"

And Paul got on his bike again. "Now I have to go back and carry sacks for that old grouch. All I do is carry sacks till my legs get bowed and my back gets bent just like Papa's. . . ."

He rode off. The gravel crunched. The larks sang. The four of them sat in the meadow next to each other rubbing their cheeks. They all looked alike: black feet in black clogs, jeans with holes in the knees, red-checked shirts, and blond tufts of hair—and on their faces expressions as mischievous as little foxes.

"Did it hurt?" I asked.

"No," said the oldest one. "It was nothing."

Then they all laughed.

They were used to getting slapped. At home they probably got slapped morning, noon, and night.

"Where do you live?" the oldest one asked.

So we went to Grandma's and drank water straight out of the tap in the barn. Grandma didn't want to give us juice.

"No," she told me, "we don't want those kids coming over here all the time. They're completely unmanageable. And things are not quite . . . as they should be . . . at home."

Later we jumped in the hay: They jumped and

I looked. I wasn't allowed to jump because of my asthma.

They were like wild animals, climbing all the way up and throwing themselves down again. They raced around and did somersaults and sometimes crashed into the walls. But they didn't care. They were used to getting hurt.

The smallest one rolled off the big haystack, yelling "Stupid, stupid!"

At just that moment Grandma passed by. She gave me a stern look, took my little brother by the hand, and pulled him along with her.

The oldest one climbed up to the very top of the haystack and was just about to throw himself down when he discovered the old carriage room on the other side. Inside the enclosure stood the old buggy which they used to hitch the horses to in the old days when riding to church. Nowadays, the buggy was never taken out, and most of the time the horse stood around in the barn.

"Look!" the oldest one shouted. All of them disappeared down the other side of the haystack.

I held my nose and climbed over the stack, too. If I got too close to hay I'd start sneezing and then I could hardly breathe.

On the other side stood the buggy. The four of them were already up in it. One of them yelled, "Bang, bang, bang," and kept shooting in all directions.

"It's a stagecoach," said the oldest one.

"What's a stagecoach?" the youngest one asked.

"It's like a bus. You pay and then you can go for a ride. . . ."

I climbed on.

At my other grandmother's, my mother's mother, we had an old dice game. All the players would get a stack of pieces of paper with stagecoaches on them; each stagecoach had room for four passengers. You'd roll the dice and get a number of passengers: Each one would be going to a different city. When you had four passengers going to the same place you could send off a stagecoach. The point was to get rid of your stagecoaches as fast as possible.

I sat alone in the backseat thinking of my other grandmother's stagecoach game. The four in front were shooting and clicking and shouting, "Whoa!"

Under the backseat, which you could lift up, was a small box. Inside was a whole stack of old schoolbooks, one of which had a list of the multiplication tables. I wanted to give that to Edwin; it would come in handy when he was figuring out how much feed to give the pigs.

There was also an old book of maps. The pages

were wavy with dampness, but the book was still usable.

The four drivers in front jumped so much that they made the buggy bounce.

"Where's the stagecoach going?" I asked.

"Where do you want to go?" asked the oldest one.

"Stockholm," I said.

"Naw!" the three younger ones said in unison.

"Then where do *you* want it to go?" I asked.

"To the swamp!" one shouted, clicking his tongue.

"To the woods!" yelled another, shooting a few Indians at the side of the road.

"To the Farmers' Cooperative!" the third one hollered. "And if that old Olofsson doesn't watch out, we'll run him over!"

They were actually nice! I had to tell Cilla. They weren't killers at all. They were nice, but they were lively and liked to fool around and couldn't sit still for very long.

Soon they got tired of the stagecoach and started jumping in the hay again. Then they raced into the barn and threw potatoes at the big boar until Edwin came and bawled them out.

Then they ran off. Zigzagging, they darted across the fields; they jumped like rabbits, then dashed ahead, paused and ran some more. One of them sang so loudly you could hear it from far away. The little one kept cursing, "Stupid, stupid, stupid."

Afterward, Grandma gave me juice and cake.

"They're different," Grandma said. "Not your kind at all."

I gave Edwin the multiplication tables.

"It was strange," I said. "We were sitting in the

same stagecoach, but we were all going to different places. . . ."

"That's the way it is," said Edwin. "That's the way it is, you know."

6

Who'll Kiss the Pig?

In the middle of the summer Grandma had a birthday. She gave a big party, and the whole family came—as well as all the neighbors, and lots of people from town.

My little brother stood by the door, shouting, "There's an old man coming! And there's another one!"

But he couldn't speak clearly yet, so no one understood what he was saying.

Even some distant relatives came from as far away as Stockholm, singing:

Happy birthday to you,
Happy birthday to you,

Happy birthday, dear Grandma,
Happy seventieth birthday to you!

They talked in loud voices and kissed everybody. The neighbors were shy; they stood in place
shuffling their feet, their jackets all buttoned up.
They shook hands and greeted each other in a serious way.

Mama and Papa were at the party, too. Papa
sat talking to an old aunt about things I couldn't
understand, and Mama stood in the kitchen putting little sandwiches on a big tray. It was during
the summer when my little brother and I lived at
Grandma's house while Mama and Papa were
building a house in town. By this time they said
they had just finished putting the roofbeams in
place.

Wearing a new brown-and-white dress that felt
fuzzy to the touch, Grandma stood in the midst of
all the guests, surrounded like a bumblebee
queen. Though she was proud that she never
wasted a penny, she said that when you gave a
party, you should never be stingy. So there were
four kinds of tiny, tiny sandwiches. And twelve
kinds of cookies. And puffy pastries with icing.
And strawberry tarts. And coffee in many, many
pitchers. And soft drinks for the children. And a
brandy punch and cigars for the men.

Even though the punch was supposed to have

been saved until later, the distant relatives, started drinking it and singing happy songs. The neighbors stood by stiffly, looking very embarrassed.

My Uncle Gustav wore a black suit. His tie was crooked and his face was red and he was sweating. Although he'd combed his hair with water, it still had bits of straw in it. Out of his ears grew little tufts of hair. His powerful arms bulged through his jacket sleeves. His big watch looked like a funny little decoration on his thick wrist. He stood talking to the neighbors about the crops, weather, and the rain that wouldn't come.

Edwin mostly kept to himself.

That was how the party began. Then Mama started to serve everyone little ham sandwiches. The distant relatives asked for beer, and nibbled at their sandwiches. But Uncle Gustav stuffed whole sandwiches into his mouth while complaining about the price of potatoes at the Farmers' Cooperative. And Cousin Cilla drank soft drinks until it looked as if she was about to choke. Then Mama brought in three other kinds of sandwiches, little towers that would fall into your lap if you didn't balance them carefully. And then came the cookies. And more coffee. And the strawberry tarts. And the speeches.

My Uncle Gustav said, "Little Mama, you've

always been so capable and clever. You've had to be thrifty your whole life. You've had to turn every last penny. Now let's have another piece of strawberry tart, little Mama, but this time make sure you don't turn that, too! Ha ha ha!"

Uncle Gustav neighed like a horse, his tie as tight as a harness around his neck.

Others made speeches, too: A neighbor and another farmer and the head of the congregation and the minister of the Pentecostal Society. They just talked and talked and talked.

In the middle of the speeches the distant relatives jumped up with arms and legs flapping, spilled the brandy punch all over the tablecloth, and, with tears in their eyes, tried to kiss Grandma.

Embarrassed, the head of the congregation cleared his throat loudly.

I went out into the barn.

There everything was the same as usual.

The boar lay sleeping in his narrow stall. The piglets were inside today; it was probably too hot to be outside. They were running around the big sow and nosing at each other. Then they ran around some more and started nuzzling again. The boar sighed deeply and tried to turn in his cramped pen, but he couldn't.

The horse was standing in his stall, staring vacantly out the window.

The cow stalls were empty. The flies buzzed around. A swallow flew up under the rafters.

The horse stomped around a bit and shifted his weight and stared out the window.

The boar sighed.

The flies buzzed. It wasn't any fun to be an animal. Everything was always the same. No birthdays. No parties. Only grits and water in the same old troughs.

I went back into the kitchen. The party hummed and roared from the parlor; everyone was talking at the same time. My Uncle Gustav was complaining about the deer that had gotten into his oat field. My cousin Cilla burped, but no one noticed.

Grandma sounded sad. "If only my beloved husband were alive today."

I put three ham sandwiches on a platter. Then I put ten cookies in my pocket, mostly the kinds called Finnish Sticks and Dreams. I set the platter with the sandwiches in front of the boar. He raised himself onto his front legs while his back end still was in the hay. Dully he stared into the trough, but in half a second he'd gobbled up all three sandwiches. Then he bit the platter, rattled it, and grunted, displeased. He sighed, and his front end sank into place again.

I took all the cookies out of my pocket and put them into the trough for the sow and her piglets. The piglets were quickest; they ate everything before the sow even got to her feet. By the time she began to search gloomily through the trough, they were quarreling over the last crumbs.

Then she grunted at me. I dug into my pockets but had nothing left. She looked so disappointed. She wasn't just sad—her little red eyes seemed to say: It isn't so strange that everything is gone; I *never* get anything!

I felt sorry for her.

Then I made up my mind. Did anyone ever kiss a sow? Did anyone kiss a pig?

I bent down. The sow looked me straight in the eye. Her snout moved back and forth. She was sniffing me like a dog.

I came closer.

Now her snout stopped moving. Her eyes didn't move. Only a few long, pale hairs on her nose quivered a little.

I kissed her.

For one lightning-quick second I felt her cold, damp snout against my mouth. A slightly musty smell streamed out of her nostrils. The long hairs tickled my cheek.

The kiss lasted just one split second.

Then the sow jumped as though I'd kicked her. She moved away as far as she could, pressing herself against the wall at the far end of the stall. The piglets squealed as they scurried out of her way. She shook her head so that her long ears wouldn't cover her tiny, red, surprised eyes.

"Little pig, you're so capable, so . . ."

She jumped again and backed farther into the corner.

Old Brutus the horse hadn't paid any attention to what had happened; he just stood staring out the window. Now he shifted his weight again. And took another look out the window.

No one ever used Brutus anymore. He was old and hardly ever got outside.

"I'm not afraid of pigs," I told him. "I'm not afraid anymore. I'm even brave enough to kiss them. . . ."

Brutus looked at me and slowly blinked his eyes.

"I'm not afraid of horses, either," I said. "They're nice. And I feel sorry for them."

Brutus stared out the window.

And suddenly it was clear to me that Brutus wanted to go for a walk. Why else did he stand looking out the window all day?

I unfastened the leather strap tied to a hook on the wall. Then I opened the stall door.

"There, little horsie, now you and I are going for a walk. . . ."

I held him by the leather halter around his neck as he trotted smartly along. Even though I stretched as much as I could, I still had to walk on tiptoe next to him.

"I'm not afraid of horses. . . ."

But then he snorted suddenly, and my heart started to pound. I opened the barn door; the sun was so bright it blinded me. We stood for a little while in the doorway. He was big, bigger than our tractor. His legs were as thick as telephone poles. His tail flapped eagerly. He scraped his shoes against the cement floor and peered out of his big eyes. I held on to the the halter; his muscles were rippling under his smooth, brown hide.

"We'll take just a little walk," I said.

Brutus snorted and scraped his hooves. His body shook, and he started to push through the door. He was so wide that I could only just fit next to him.

"There, there," I said, trying to calm him down.

But he didn't hear me. His ears were twitching. His eyes were wide open, his nostrils quivered and he was breathing heavily.

Then he took off into the yard, his hooves sending a spray of gravel in all directions. He snorted and shook his big head. I held on to the halter, but he lifted me right off the ground. He danced around and around in the yard. I clung to the halter, only touching ground with every other step. His legs pumped up and down like a machine, and I was afraid of getting caught beneath them.

We headed onto the road. I lost my grip and fell at the edge of the ditch. But Brutus kept running, his head held high; his big, heavy body seemed to bounce down the dirt road.

"Stop, stop, stop!" I shouted.

But he didn't.

Far down the road he pulled up, just at the edge of the oat field. He sniffed and slowly walked into the field as though he were walking into cold water. Then he started to eat.

I ran after him into the oat field, picked up the halter and started to pull. He was calm now. He didn't look up, didn't pay attention to me, just ate deliberately as if he had decided to eat up the whole field before evening came.

I pulled and pulled, but it was like moving a whole house.

He wouldn't budge.

*   *   *

Then I saw Grandma alone in the garden under the cherry tree dressed in her fuzzy brown-and-white dress. Probably she'd come there to get away from all the noise and commotion. Maybe she wanted to have some peace and quiet to think about Grandpa.

"Grandma! Grandma!" I shouted.

She saw me and ran toward me with her arms waving like bumblebee wings.

"Hey! What are you doing, boy?"

She walked into the field, grabbed Brutus's halter, and pulled as hard as she could. But Brutus wouldn't budge. So she picked a big bunch of oats and put it in his mouth. Then she pulled again.

The horse followed her.

"Boy! Boy!" Grandma said sternly.

We walked back to the barn.

"I wanted him to have a little fun, too, on your birthday. . . ."

The horse trotted obligingly into the barn. Grandma locked him in his stall and tied the halter to the hook in the wall.

That's when she noticed the platter lying in the boar's trough.

I told her the whole story—even that I'd kissed the big sow.

66

She squatted next to me on the barn floor.

"Perhaps a person has to kiss a pig once in his life to really understand them." She nodded. Then she hugged me.

"But did you really do it?" She laughed. "What was it *like?*"

She sounded very curious.

7

The Oak Tree,
the Rocks,
and the Place Where
You Can Rest Your Legs

On Saturday afternoons Edwin would walk to the library in town. Even though it wasn't open on weekends, the schoolteacher would let him in. He would sit and read for a few hours, and then walk home again. He never borrowed any books.

"What do you read?" I asked, sitting beside him on his bed.

"History," he replied. "Things that happened many hundreds of years ago, see. Napoleon, the French Revolution, the great wars, Louis XIV. . . ."

He was sitting close to me. He smelled a little

funny, like the insides of old gloves.

Edwin had a little room in Grandma's house. There wasn't any wallpaper, just bare plank walls. He had a narrow bed, a simple writing table, some notebooks where he could write down things he wanted to remember, two pens in a case. His dress-up clothes hung on nails in the wall. Above the writing table was a picture of his mother when she was young. Nothing else.

"I read about kings, see. About the elegant life at court. If you could just imagine what it was like inside a castle, with the big rooms, the gilded wallpaper, carved furniture, ladies in pretty clothes. . . . On one tile stove they even painted a thousand tiny pictures of a king, see!"

He stood up, pointing as if he were standing right inside the castle.

"I read it all in books," he said.

It was the summer that my little brother and I lived with Grandma while Mama and Papa were building a house for us in town. It was August, and they were putting tiles on the roof.

"You know what we can do?" said Edwin. "You can go with me—that way you'll understand why I read books. . . ."

I asked Grandma for permission. She was sitting by the radio, thumbing through the

Pentecostal Times. I leaned over her shoulder.

"Go ahead, boy," she said.

"Don't you want to go with us?"

"No, I don't read books. They're not for the likes of me."

I looked at the pictures in her newspaper of poor children in Addis Ababa. They were sitting under a big tree doing their lessons. There was another picture of a fat lady with a big wart on her chin cooking porridge for the poor children.

Then we started off. Edwin was wearing a gray jacket and blue pants. He had taken off his cap and put on a beret. We walked down the road, warmed by the afternoon sun.

"Why do you read?" I asked.

"To understand," said Edwin.

"But you understand everything already! You know about everything."

"No."

"Pigs and beets!"

"Five times five," said Edwin, laughing. "Is that what you mean?"

"Twenty-five," I answered.

"But pigs and beets aren't everything. There's so much more—the whole world, the history of the world. I want to understand all of it, really *understand* it. You have to understand the world, you have to understand history, see?"

We walked down the dusty road to town. Edwin walked quickly, and I scampered after him.

"Books!" he said. "Books!"

The library door was locked, but the school-teacher lived right next door. Edwin went over and knocked quietly on the door. No one answered.

I shaded my eyes with my hands and peered through the library window. Inside, it was dark and gloomy. I could just make out the open shelves with hundreds of books, all with their backs to me.

Edwin knocked again, but still no one answered.

"I think he's taking a nap," he said disappointedly.

"Should we wake him up?"

"No, I wouldn't do that to him. We'll have to come back next Saturday."

So we headed home again. Halfway there we came to a big oak tree growing by the side of the road. Underneath it were two big rocks. We sat in the shade and rested our legs for a while.

Edwin went on telling me about the castle and about wars and revolutions and the old days.

"But why do you read about all that old stuff?" I asked.

"Old stuff? Don't start thinking that history is just old stuff!"

History, I thought to myself. Isn't that things that happened a really long time ago, before cars and tractors, flashlights or radios?

"Nothing is old, see."

The oak we were sitting under was at least three hundred years old, he said. They had chopped down one as big as this one by the church, and had studied it to see how old it was.

"Three hundred years ago," he said, "when this tree was just a small plant next to the big rocks, do you know what it was like. . . ?

"At that time southern Sweden, where we live now, was Danish. Then Sweden and Denmark had a war, and the Danes lost. Everyone who lived here suddenly became Swedish. . . .'.

"When the oak tree grew a little bigger, perhaps about fifteen feet tall, it was during the reign of Karl XII. In France, Louis XIV lived in the castle at Versailles, and beautiful ladies wore fancy dresses and soldiers wore beautiful uniforms—and their horses wore plumes.

"Then came the eighteenth century. By then the oak tree was maybe twenty-four feet tall, a nice little tree.

"Then the French Revolution and the Revolutionary War in America. That was long before the battles between the Indians and settlers that you kids play.

"And then the nineteenth century. By now the oak was about forty-five feet tall, a big tree.

"Napoleon could have sat under this very tree. And Beethoven, who wrote music. That was also when they invented the steam engine.

"Then came the twentieth century. By then the oak was sixty feet tall. There were two great wars. Thousands of discoveries and inventions. For the oak it was all like yesterday. . . ."

He patted the rough bark of the oak tree.

"This old oak was standing here before people knew how the world worked. At a time when they burned witches at the stake. This oak tree was a *big* tree in the eighteenth century when Linneaus wrote his book about how plants reproduce."

He paused. "Old, you talk about old. Just look at this rock you're sitting on. It must have come from a mountain far up North. The glacier took it right out of a mountain, carried it and put it here, in the middle of the field, a long, long time ago— a thousand years before the Stone Age."

He patted the rock he was sitting on, and some moss fell off.

"Ho, ho, ho, there could be runes written under the moss carved by someone more than a thousand years ago."

I looked carefully, but all I saw were some wood lice scampering away.

"Ho, ho, these rocks have been here since history began. And the rocks are so big that no one could move them even though they're in a field. And because they couldn't be moved, no one cut down the oak tree. And because the oak tree makes shade and the rocks are good for sitting on, you and I stopped here and rested a while. The rocks, the oak tree, and us. It all fits together. We're a tiny, tiny part of history, you and I, this very moment, see."

The sun filtered through the crown of the tree, where birds were singing and insects buzzing.

"How tall is the oak tree?" I asked.

"Seventy-five feet—or about twenty-five yards, see," said Edwin. "Do you know how to find out?"

"I guess you'd have to get Grandma's measuring tape and climb up to the thinnest branches," I said.

"No, that would be too hard, see. But you can measure the shadow. Come on!"

We walked into the sun, and Edwin paced off my shadow. It was two yards long.

"And you're about one yard—or about three feet—tall," he said. "That means that your shadow is twice your size at the moment. If I were to measure the shadow of the oak tree in the field, then I could figure out how tall the oak tree is, too. Understand?"

He went back to the tree trunk and started pacing off the distance with long steps. He walked across the road and into the field, counting out loud.

"Twenty-three, twenty-four . . . Here's the French Revolution!"

He walked straight into the cabbage patch toward the spot where the highest branches of the oak tree were casting their shadows.

"Thirty-one, thirty-two . . . The steam engine!"

From far down the road a dust cloud was coming toward us. When it got closer I saw that it was the truck from the Farmers' Cooperative. Paul was driving, and Olofsson was sitting next to him.

"Forty-four. The First World War. Forty-five. The Second World War! Forty-six. Right now!"

Edwin spread his arms and turned toward me.

The truck pulled to a screeching halt, and Olofsson rolled down the window; his face was red and his eyes black.

"What do you think you're doing, you big oaf? Taking a walk in the Farmers' Cooperative cabbage patch! Just who do you think you *are?*"

Paul sniggered, and Olofsson rolled the window back up. The truck disappeared in a cloud of smoke.

"It's seventy feet—or about twenty-three yards tall, see. And three hundred years old."

8

All the Dead

My little brother was the most stubborn kid I ever saw. He also couldn't speak clearly enough for people to understand him.

One day he was lying in the grass underneath the cherry tree, being stubborn. He kept shouting something that sounded like: "Uu ouus ow!"

I was taking care of him while Grandma sat in the kitchen arranging old photographs.

I got mad at him.

"If you don't keep quiet, I'll call the police," I said.

"Uu ouus o-w-w!" he hollered.

I couldn't stand him.

"I don't *like* you," I said in a serious voice. "Don't think for a moment that I do. . . ."

He pulled his hat over his eyes and howled.

Then Grandma came out and said, "Whatever is the matter, little one?"

But he just kept crying, and pulled big clumps of grass out of the lawn.

Finally he fell asleep. Grandma put the little monster in his bed.

"He should have had his nap earlier," Grandma said. "He gets so overtired."

It was an afternoon in August during the summer when my little brother and I lived at Grandma's while Papa and Mama were building a house in town. Now they were installing pipes and putting in faucets. That's what they told us.

When my little brother was fast asleep, Grandma gathered up her photographs and put them into a small box.

"I'll show them to Gunhild next time I go there," she said. "Listen, what do you say we go and visit her now? Edwin can look after the baby. . . ."

So we went. My grandma's sister Gunhild lived in the Old People's Home in town. Grandma brought along a bouquet of dahlias and the box of photographs. We took the shortcut along bumpy cowpaths through the light woods and the dark woods. Through the oak and elm woods with cheerfully chattering birds, and through the spruce woods with the wind sighing mournfully in the treetops.

The Old People's Home was a gloomy-looking brick building in between the savings bank and the offices of the town government. As I went up the stairs, the hallway echoed, and it felt cold.

The crazy people lived on the second floor. I peeked in through the glass double doors and saw two old men in gray jackets sitting there. One of the men had slid down so that he was almost lying on his back in his armchair; every once in a while he screamed as if he was stuck. The other man sat stiffly, babbling. His eyes stared straight ahead, and he had saliva on his chin.

I ran over to Grandma and held her hand.

"Don't be afraid, little one. They're nice, both of them, but things are not so easy for them."

I thought it was horrible.

"Let's thank God that we're all right. . . ."

The old people lived on the third floor. We went into a room that had two empty beds and a view of the garden. Grandma first greeted a little old lady with bright brown eyes.

Gunhild was sitting in her bed with a cover over her, plucking at the sheets. On the wall was a piece of cloth with a picture of an old man and woman on it. Grandma told me that underneath the picture it said "OLD LOVE DOES NOT DIE."

On the night table were some asters that were beginning to wither. Grandma changed the flowers.

"How are you doing, Gunhild?" Grandma said loudly.

"Oi, oi, oi," said Gunhild, never once looking at us.

I didn't like to look at her. She looked so much like Grandma, only more wrinkled, and her face didn't move at all—it was as if she had completely stopped thinking.

"I brought flowers. And the boy came along, too."

She didn't look either at me or the flowers.

"Oi, oi, oi," she said.

The lady who lived with Gunhild—the spry little old lady—kept walking around. She pinched dead leaves off the flowers in her vase and smoothed out her bedspread for the third time.

"She's not so well today," she said, going over to the window and opening it.

Grandma took her old photographs out of the box. There were pictures of old uncles and cousins, old photographs whose edges had been nibbled at by mice.

80

"She's not well. She can't look at pictures," said the spry old lady, and she smoothed out the bedspread and went to shut the window.

"Oh, sure she can," said Grandma sharply.

The little old lady left the room.

"Do you remember these old pictures?" said Grandma, chuckling.

Gunhild said something I couldn't understand. It sounded like "aa-uu."

"Yes, that's Uncle Arthur," Grandma said. "I found the pictures in a drawer."

"Jeanna," Gunhild said, pointing at the picture.

"That's right," Grandma said. "That was the name of Hans's horse. Now I remember."

"Arthur?" Gunhild said, searching her memory.

"He's dead," Grandma said. She knew exactly what Gunhild was thinking. "He died in forty-eight, don't you remember? It was raining so hard at the funeral, and old Elna dropped her umbrella right down on the coffin. . . ."

"Oh, yes, I remember that," Gunhild said.

She leafed through the photographs and pulled out a picture of old Elna with her son.

"Erik?" Gunhild asked. "Isn't he a policeman?"

Now she was speaking quite normally. She

could smile again, and her face moved in the usual way.

"Erik's dead," Grandma said. "He died last summer. The funeral was on the fourth of July. I just sent flowers. . . ."

"I hope you sent flowers for me, too."

"Yes, I wrote from both of us."

"That's good."

I sat on the floor, listening, as they went through the whole pile of photographs. There was Karl, straight as a ramrod in his black coat and top hat. And Nils-Gustav in his vest looking like a moron, with his mouth hanging open. And Aunt Emmy with a tiny bird of a hat on her head. They were all dead.

For an hour they sat talking and helping each other remember.

"What happened to little Oscar?"

"Oh, he died year before last."

"You don't say!"

"And what about Big Brother Edward?"

"He died many years ago. Cancer."

"You don't say!"

They only talked about people who were dead. One after the other. All Gunhild could say was, "You don't say!"

Then we left. In the hallway the spry old lady

was pacing restlessly.

"A little patience helps a lot!" said Grandma.

The spry old lady didn't answer.

By the time we got back, my little brother had woken up. He was sitting in his bed sobbing. For some reason I felt sorry for him.

"Uu ouww oow," he said.

I sat down next to him.

"What did you say?"

"Uu ouww oow."

"What's ouww?" I asked.

Surprised, he looked at me and pointed to his jacket and sweater.

He wanted to put on more clothes. "Put clothes on." Well, that was the typical kind of idea that little kids get. But if he wanted them, it was okay with me.

I put one sweater on him, then another. Then his jacket. I pulled his little cap down so that it covered his ears.

In a split second he was as happy as a lark. We walked over to the hedge to look at ants—or rather he rolled along, fat as a sausage but very

pleased with himself. We sat by the hedge and started to talk to the ants. I felt so sorry for my little, little brother.

I sang:

> *When it's raining, come to me*
> *I'll always protect you.*

Sweat was pouring down his face. And flies were buzzing around him.

> *When a fly buzzes around you*
> *I'll catch it in my hand.*
> *You shouldn't be afraid*
> *'Cause I'm by your side.*

I couldn't catch a single fly, but I sang on:

> *I'll be a real big brother to you*
> *I'll carry you on my back for many miles.*
> *When you are cold, come to me*
> *I'll always warm you up.*

I hugged him. By now he was panting, and he could hardly move in all the sweaters; he was so hot that I actually had to blow on him to cool him off.

9

The Sad Death
of Emma the Pig

While Uncle Gustav and Edwin prepared for butchering, I went into the barn.

There everything was as still and quiet as usual. The horse stood munching oats in his stall. The boar was asleep. The piglets—who now were as big as dogs—bustled around in their sty. In their midst lay Emma the pig. When I came in, she grunted dejectedly.

"Poor, poor Emma," I said. "In ten minutes you won't be here anymore."

This was during the summer when my little brother and I lived at Grandma's while Papa and Mama were building a house for us in town. At this point an electrician was helping them put in all the wires for the fixtures and the electric stove.

It was almost fall by now. Sometime in September. Late in the afternoon. All day long Uncle Gustav and Edwin had been riding the combine-harvester. Soon the cows would be driven home for milking. And in between harvesting and milking Emma was to be butchered.

It was windy outside; the treetops bowed in the wind. The cherry tree was losing its leaves. The weather was gloomy, and a little cold. The asters looked bright red in their flower beds.

In the middle of the yard Edwin had placed a wooden bench, and three buckets of scalding-hot water stood there steaming. Two enameled buckets were standing next to them. On the ground lay three knives and a whetstone. And a heavy sledgehammer.

Everything was ready.

"Poor, poor Emma," I said.

She stood up, shook her head, and grunted something. The piglets nuzzled her. The boar in his stall sighed heavily, still fast asleep.

Edwin came in. It was time.

He opened the gate and walked over to the stall.

Emma pulled back. The piglets climbed all over each other.

"Come on now, little pig," Edwin said. "It'll be over soon. . . ."

Edwin had a rope in his hand. When Emma had backed all the way into the corner he put the loop around her neck. Then he pulled her out with him.

Emma screamed and tried to resist by stiffening her legs. She dug in her feet and slid along the floor, hay and chaff flying all around her.

Edwin stopped to catch his breath, then started pulling again.

"They know when it's time, see. It's strange, but animals feel these things."

Outside stood Uncle Gustav, sharpening the knives. Edwin dragged out Emma the pig, shutting the barn door behind him.

The pig howled and tried to run toward the field and the woods, but Edwin held on tight. Gustav helped him, and together they got the pig onto the bench. There she lay on her stomach across the bench with all four legs still touching the ground.

"That's it, that's it," said Uncle Gustav. "That's just right."

Now the pig was lying completely still. She'd given up; she was just waiting.

"She's fat and fine," said Uncle Gustav. "She'll make good bacon."

He took the sledgehammer and lifted it.

I wanted to shout something, but couldn't.

I felt so terrible for her. She hadn't even been
allowed to say good-bye to her piglets. Or to the
old boar. She'd just been dragged off.

She closed her eyes for a moment. Then looked
up again. Her ears trembled. Otherwise, she lay
completely still, just waiting.

Animals have to be butchered. How else can people get food? Raising animals and butchering them: That's what a farmer does.

There were two other sows in the barn, and twenty-five piglets. Emma was too old. She couldn't have babies anymore, so one of the piglets would have to take her place . . . and old Emma would become food for us.

The pig shivered a little. Uncle Gustav raised the sledgehammer.

She squealed in a way I'd never heard pigs squeal. And her squeal echoed back and forth between the house and the stables, between the barn and the chicken coop, and then disappeared across the fields and out toward the woods.

I turned my head away. All I could hear was her feet scratching a little at the ground. Then it was quiet.

I peeked out again. I had a lump in my throat. It was so disgusting and sad. And yet it was the only thing to do.

Emma lay motionless on the bench. Where the sledgehammer had hit her in the middle of her forehead was a bloody mark. She was unconscious.

"Hu ha," said Uncle Gustav, setting down the sledgehammer. "This is no fun."

Edwin moved Emma so that her head hung

over the edge of the bench. He dragged over one of the buckets and placed it under her neck.

I hadn't noticed that Aunt Anna had come out into the yard. Now she said, "I'm ready."

And with one single slash Edwin cut open the pig's neck. I felt sick and had to turn away.

When I looked again, Aunt Anna and Edwin were draining the blood, first into one bucket, then into another.

Then the blood stopped. The pig was drained dry. The pig's front leg quivered a little. Then she was still.

Edwin took the hot water and poured it over the body.

He poured out all three buckets. The body on the bench steamed and smoked. One of the knives was a razor, which he used to scrape away all the dirt and long bristles. After fifteen minutes the pig's body was smooth and white, like a newly peeled potato. You could see thin veins shining through like the blue rivers in my book of maps.

Next, Uncle Gustav fastened two hooks to the hind legs, and with block and tackle hoisted the pig so that she was hanging head down against the stable door.

Edwin cut her stomach open. All the innards tumbled out into a big wooden tub.

"Don't look so unhappy, boy," said Grandma,

who had come outside. "This isn't a sad event."

Uncle Gustav and Edwin got another big wooden tub. Then they started cutting. First they cut off the feet and put them in a tub. Then the head, the shoulder, and the chops. Uncle Gustav and Edwin carried everything into Aunt Anna's kitchen. Then they cleaned up.

That evening, after milking, we all sat in the kitchen. Aunt Anna had fried a little of the bacon with sugar and salt until it was crisp and crunchy, and she served it for supper. Uncle Gustav got to eat the curly tail.

They looked at me.

"Don't feel so bad," said Grandma. "Everyone has to eat. Or else we'd all starve."

My little brother was sitting in her lap. He'd been asleep.

I remembered all the starving children in Addis Ababa.

"But what about all the starving children in Africa? Will there be enough for them, too?"

Uncle Gustav laughed. He was holding the curly tail between his teeth; his face was greasy.

"Sure there will," he said. "That was some fat old pig. Ha ha ha. But let's eat now. . . ."

I tasted the bacon. Very, very cautiously. It was good. And I was hungry.

10

If They Didn't Have Me . . .

It was tall. I was standing by Grandma's window, looking out. It was windy; the trees were swaying, and the dead rose vine outside the window was rattling back and forth against the wall. Dry leaves whirled around on the ground, heading toward the woodshed and the rabbit hutches and back to the gooseberry bushes and into the road as though the wind couldn't make up its mind where to put them. The sky was dark. Sullen black rain clouds rushed across the sky.

I shivered a little. Grandma was knitting and my little brother was sleeping. On the radio a man was talking in a shrill, blaring voice.

This happened when my little brother and I lived at Grandma's house while Papa and Mama were building a house in town. Now a man was putting in the floor, they said. Would that house *ever* be done?

I stood by the window looking out. I was homesick, or else I wished I were somewhere else, or . . . I don't know.

I went out to the cow barn. Grandma didn't notice that I'd left; her knitting needles clicked on, and the man on the radio kept talking in his loud, excited voice.

In the cow barn everything was as usual. The horse stared drowsily through the window like a tired, old uncle. The boar was asleep in his stall with his ears folded over his eyes. The piglets were squirming around in their own pen. The same as usual, everything was the same as usual.

"But what about Emma?" I said angrily to the piglets. "Your mama is dead. She's been butchered. Aren't you sad?"

They weren't. They didn't care. It made no difference to them if their mama had disappeared. As long as they had grits to slurp down and water to splash in, they didn't care at all.

I felt empty somehow, abandoned, so lonely and sad.

I went out to the yard and headed toward Uncle Gustav's house. From inside I heard voices. Uncle Gustav was saying, "Ain't that the darndest . . . ha ha ha . . ."

I knew that there was a potato salesman visiting him. I peeked in the window. The barrel-shaped salesman, whose name was Jonsson, was wearing a black jacket with dandruff on the shoulders. In his rough hands was a thick, thick wallet held together with a rubber band. When he said something, my Uncle Gustav laughed again:

"Ain't that the darndest . . . ha ha ha."

He was laughing on the other side of the window. I felt even more abandoned and lonely.

I trudged down toward the woodshed, kicking piles of leaves as I went. I sang quietly to myself:

If they didn't have me
Would they even miss me?
If they didn't have me
Would they even be sad?
Or would they just smile and laugh
As if nothing had happened at all?

Suddenly I decided to run away. I was standing by the woodshed and the rabbit hutches when I said out loud, "See you, rabbits!"

They didn't care about me. They were sitting with their backs against the wire mesh. The black one was asleep, and the two white ones were busy eating; they had no time for me. Their frightened babies lay in the farthest corner of the hutch as still as little toy animals.

"See you, rabbits!" I repeated.

They didn't even turn around. So I left.

I walked across the rye field, which had turned into a stubby mat after harvesting.

I walked past the light woods, which were now growing sparser every day, and into the dark woods. The earth was springy, and the doves cooed desolately. It was dark and cool: In here it was never summer, spring, or fall—it was always deep, dark, and gloomy. Here things never changed.

Even though I scratched myself on sharp branches, I walked faster and faster because I started to think that the cooing doves were really big, dangerous hoot owls. I stumbled over hidden roots and staggered along like a drunkard.

Far into the forest, in a half-overgrown glade, was a deserted farmhouse. At one end the roof had caved in and the windows were broken. The door slammed back and forth in the wind. I walked inside.

The floor was covered with trash. A torn sofa, some empty sacks, some mousetraps without springs, and gravel and dove droppings. The wallpaper was ripped; underneath I could see the

bricks. When I touched them, they felt as cold as
loneliness.

Silently I sang:

> *Now they don't have me*
> *I hope that they're sorry.*
> *Now that I'm gone*
> *I want them to cry.*

But I wondered if they were really crying.

I could actually hear how my Uncle Gustav had
gone on with that Jonsson, the one with the fat
wallet. I could actually hear Uncle Gustav cack-
ling, "Ain't that the darndest. Ha ha ha."

Then I sang:

> *Now they don't have me*
> *But I don't suppose they care. . . .*

A door creaked. A howling sound came from the chimney pipe. I thought I saw something move in the empty sacks on the floor. I ran out as fast as I could, off toward town.

I ran so fast that my asthma started to bother me; it got harder and harder to breathe, and I had to stop by the graveyard. Suddenly there was a hole in the black clouds, and the sun came out for a moment; it felt a little warmer. I went through the gate under one of the giant oak trees that had stood there for three hundred years, for many long generations.

The paths were neatly raked. The gravel crunched beneath my shoes. I walked past rows of gravestones with the names of dead people on them, but I could read only the shortest ones: Anna, Karl, Erik. I knew that there was a star next to the date they were born, and a cross next to the date they'd died. Star. Cross. Star. Cross.

On top of the gravestones were little carved stone doves, doves from the dark forest, doves with their gloomy cooing.

Here they all were. All the dead. Wrinkled old men with watery eyes who'd died, old ladies with shaking hands who'd died. There were even little children who'd died, Grandma had told me. Some who'd maybe swum too far out in the ponds when they really hadn't known how to swim. Some who'd maybe petted some strange dogs and been bitten to death. Some who'd maybe felt abandoned and said, "See you, rabbits," and run away. Maybe. . . .

The sun warmed my back, but my thoughts made me cold inside. It was like a pain, like a cold knife in my chest.

Just graves, graves, graves. Dead people in long rows. Did anyone miss them? Did anyone think about them sometimes, feel a sudden pang of sadness in the midst of their happiness, and maybe even cry a bit? Did they?

An old man was standing by a grave, standing completely still with his hat in his hand. Still, and as sad as a horse in a meadow in the rain. I snuck right by him; he didn't notice me at all.

At the end of the row the gravedigger had dug a new grave. It was a big, deep rectangle in the black dirt and clay. On all sides were planks so that people's feet wouldn't cave in the edges. I sat down on the planks and dangled my feet into the grave. It was still hard to breathe.

This is the last stop, I thought to myself. Sooner or later we will all go to this place. It isn't so far from home. . . .

I wasn't sure exactly how long I stayed away.

Maybe an hour, maybe many. I don't know how long I sat on the plank, looking down into the grave. Maybe quite a while.

All at once I heard someone shout my name. It was coming from far away.

I waited.

Then I heard the shout again. Someone was shouting loudly from the farm, probably with hands around his mouth like a trumpet. Another voice came from the dark woods; both were shouting my name.

I waited a while.

Then there was more shouting. Two more voices from the farm—one was Grandma's, the other could have been Mama's. Then two voices from the direction of the dark woods—Uncle Gustav's and maybe Aunt Anna's. One voice rumbled all the way up from the swamp: It almost sounded like Papa's. And one voice was quite close. It had to be Edwin.

I answered.

"Yes-s."

The voice kept shouting and shouting. Coming closer and closer.

I answered again.

"Yes-s."

Then Edwin came into the graveyard. I heard the gravel crunching under his feet.

"Where have you been, boy?" he asked.

I didn't answer.

"What are you doing here?"

I didn't answer.

"Mama and Papa were worried, see."

I sat silent.

"We were all worried, see."

He stopped in the gravel and stood there a long time.

"Five times five?" he said.

"Twenty-five," I answered.

He picked me up and put me on his shoulders and hurried toward home.

"Why did you run away?"

"I don't know," I said. "I wanted to see if you cared about me. . . ."

"Well then, do you think we cared about you?" he asked, and laughed.

He paused. They were calling, "Yoo hoo! Where are you?" from all directions.

"I found him," screamed Edwin.

Then all the voices fell silent. Edwin galloped toward home. In the light woods I had to huddle low so that I wouldn't hit my head on the boughs. He didn't stop before he reached the yard, where everyone stood waiting.

"He wanted to see if we missed him," puffed Edwin.

Mama kissed me all over my face.

Grandma said, "Oi, oi, oi." Uncle Gustav laughed and hugged Aunt Anna.

Papa threw me gently into the air a few times.

"The house'll be ready soon, son!"

11

The Lonesome Pilot

I got to see Cilla's room only once. On the very last day.

I walked through the front hallway where Uncle Gustav's muddy boots and all their clogs were lined up on newspapers on the floor. The cat rubbed herself lovingly against my leg. I walked through the kitchen and through the parlor where all the knickknacks were lined up as if they were in a museum. Then up the steep, narrow attic staircase, and to the left.

"Who is it?" she shouted from inside.

"Me."

Carefully she unlocked the door, looked swiftly in all directions, pulled me in, and locked the door again quickly. It was very secretive and exciting.

Inside, the room was a mess. Even though it was late in the afternoon, the bed wasn't made. On the floor were apple cores, clothes, old news-

papers, candy wrappers, books, and parts of an old radio that she said she was going to fix.

"What do you do up here all day?" I asked.

"Read." She snorted.

"What do you read?"

I picked up her book from the floor and tried to read it. Edwin had just begun to teach me. But the words were too close together.

She pulled the book out of my hands and was about to start reading again.

It was the only time I got to visit Cilla's room the whole time my little brother and I lived at Grandma's house while Mama and Papa were building a house in town.

I enjoyed being upstairs in all that jumble. Carefully I sat down on the bed. Cilla cleared her throat and began to read.

Captain Anderson took the plane down to 2000 feet. The old bomber was flying over a beautiful English landscape. The sun was just going down; a light mist hung over the fields. The cows grazing in the meadows craned their necks in surprise at the great bird.

But Captain Anderson did not have time to admire the beauty of the landscape. One rudder had been shot off; one engine had stopped. And he did not know if the landing gear was working.

He heard Jack the radioman shouting into the microphone:

"One Six Zero Five to Central. This is RAF 1605. We have some problems."

"What did he shout into the microphone?" I asked.

"Oh, that's English," hissed Cilla. "That's what they always speak in the air."

She went on reading.

"If I ever get out of this, I'm going to . . . ," said Captain Anderson, but he interrupted himself when he looked down at the fuel gauge.

Not a drop left. This was it!

Below him he could see the airfield. The landing lights were blinking. The fire engine stood ready and waiting.

The navigator folded up the maps.

"We'd better say a little prayer," said Anderson.

The old bomber started its descent at a steep angle, wings shaking, engines roaring. The airfield came closer and closer. Captain Anderson broke into a sweat.

"Now I just hope we still have wheels," he said quietly.

The motors snorted and the propellers roared. The aircraft danced ahead like a wobbly bird.

106

Finally it touched ground softly, like a caress.
The landing gear creaked, but everything held.
Just then the engines died. The fuel was gone.
"We have just landed," *Jack said into the microphone in a trembling voice.*
Captain Anderson stepped out of the plane. Lolita was waiting for him. She covered him with burning kisses. The two of them had forgotten the world; they stood there completely alone among the people on the airfield. And with his hand he . . .

"No o," Cilla said.

She looked at me doubtfully. Then she shut the book.

"This isn't for little kids. You wouldn't understand it. You'd better go now."

Disappointed, I got up to leave. Cilla locked the door behind me and I heard the bed creak as she lay down again to find out what Captain Anderson did afterward. I'd never know.

I walked outside. It was cold and dark, late fall, almost winter, and it had been raining all day. Everything was soaked.

In one corner of Grandma's garden was an old shack that had once been a chicken coop but was no longer used; they'd built a new and better one. I went inside. The old book of maps I had found was lying in one of the nests. I picked it up and climbed onto the highest perches. Up there was a little window; I wiped off the dirt, spiderwebs, and chicken feathers, and looked out.

The streetlights along the road leading to the church were lit—the road looked like an airfield. Everything was ready for takeoff.

The motors snorted. The propellers roared. The big aircraft slowly taxied into the yard and past the barn. As I drove past Uncle Gustav's house, I slowed down and waved at them. Then I gave it more gas and rolled down the road toward town. As I guided the plane off the ground, I just managed to clear the church steeple: The weathervane tickled the plane's belly.

Then I flew off. Into the world. The wind tore at the old tarpaper roof. Would all the nails hold? Would all the perches stay in place? I walked around, inspecting everything. Yes, it would do.

I opened the book of maps. I was glad Edwin had taught me to read a little; you have to be able to read when you're in the air. We were on page six in the map book, Sweden. But the plane was going incredibly fast. The wind howled through all the cracks and the motors roared and the chicken droppings on the floor actually shook.

Now we were on page eight already, Central

Europe and the British Isles. Far below I could see Paris. And there was Rome! Now we were going so fast I had to crouch!

I picked up the microphone.

"Raynimack baynni booroo!" That was my code.

(In the air you always speak English.)

Then we were flying over a big ocean. I could see a fat man swimming down there, waving at me. But I set the motor at full speed ahead. We zoomed across page ten, Italy. Then to page twelve, Western Soviet Union. Then skipped to page sixteen, China, Japan, and Korea. We were going so fast that I could hardly turn the pages quickly enough. If Grandma's chicken coop was destroyed by the terrible speed, she probably wouldn't mind: She didn't need it any longer.

I walked over to one of the old nests, where there was an extra-powerful motor. I turned the buttons. With a lionlike roar, it started up. I knelt down, holding tight to the perches.

Then I shouted into the microphone: *"Mayrraybake!"*

And the aircraft shot into space like a dry leaf in the wind! I climbed up to the window and looked out.

It was incredibly beautiful. A clear blue light surrounded us, and when I saw the planet Earth off in the distance I had to sigh. It was no bigger than an apple hanging all by itself. And it was so beautiful. It looked exactly like the cover of the book of maps. With big islands, blue oceans, and tall, dirt-brown mountains.

The Earth is very beautiful from up there—that I can assure you. And I could have held it in my hand like a little apple!

I said, "Don't be afraid, everybody! Nothing bad will happen to you! I'll protect all of you! Everything will be all right! Just don't ever be afraid!"

While I stood looking out the window, I heard my mother's voice. I caught a glimpse of Mama and Papa behind the cherry tree. They were calling me, and that meant that I couldn't stay in space any longer, I had to go home; otherwise, I knew they'd worry.

I looked at my beautiful little Earth one last time.

It's a fine place to live, that I can promise you. With brown mountains to climb, as brown as dirt; you can take long, long hikes if you bring enough in your backpack to eat and drink. And there are islands to discover, big, mysterious, beautiful islands. And an ocean to swim in, a big blue ocean that you can dive into or paddle around on, if you happen to have a boat.

It's a beautiful place, that I can promise you. The finest place there is. All the other places you can see from up in space look much duller, I think, not nearly as much fun. But on Earth you never have to be bored for a moment. . . .

They were calling me again.

I turned off the extra-powerful motor and shouted into the microphone: *"Berray sum regimack!"*

The Earth grew bigger and bigger, the oceans bluer and bluer. The mountains were brown, the valleys green, and the big deserts sandy yellow.

I flew straight down to Earth. Right onto page forty-one, Northeast Africa. And there I saw Addis Ababa, and all the poor children. But they didn't look so poor anymore! As I flew by, they were sitting under the trees gobbling up fat pork chops and cookies left over from some party. They didn't even need to eat the porridge that the fat lady with the wart on her chin had made; she'd have to eat it herself. She was the only one who looked a little grumpy.

There are plenty of pigs in the world, fat and juicy like Emma: There's enough food for everyone! And as many cookies as anyone could ever want, Finnish Sticks and Dreams and I don't know what all. . . .

Mama was calling me again.

I flew as fast as I could. Over London. Across the swamp and the light woods. And I brought the plane down at a steep angle next to the church.

Then I shut the book of maps and said a little prayer.

I landed. Mama was waiting for me. She covered me with burning kisses and we forgot the world around us. We stood there completely alone among all the people on the farm, and with my hand . . . I patted her on the nose.

"Now we're going to our new home," Papa said. "Everything's ready."

"Go to Grandma and say good-bye and thank you," Mama said.

I ran off. It was dark outside; the grass and rotting leaves were soaked. But I didn't care. I sang:

> *Now I've been here a whole summer*
> *From morning till night.*
> *Now I'm going home to my house*
> *Where there's room for everyone.*
> *Room for my little brother,*
> *And also room for me,*
> *Room for Mama,*
> *Room for Papa,*
> *Room for Grandma if she wants to come,*

And for Edwin if he would come,
And for Uncle Gustav and Aunt Anna,
Where they can sit down,
And for . . .

I said the names of everyone I knew, and many more. And it became a song that went on and on and on. . . .